THE TREEHOUSE FUN BOOK

THE TREEHOUSE FUN BOOK

ANDY GRIFFITHS
JILL GRIFFITHS
and **TERRY DENTON**

SQUARE
FISH

Feiwel and Friends • New York

SQUARE FISH

An imprint of Macmillan Publishing Group, LLC
175 Fifth Avenue
New York, NY 10010
mackids.com

Square Fish and the Square Fish logo are trademarks of Macmillan and
are used by Feiwel and Friends under license from Macmillan.

Our books may be purchased in bulk for promotional, educational, or business
use. Please contact your local bookseller or the Macmillan Corporate and
Premium Sales Department at (800) 221-7945 ext. 5442 or by e-mail
at MacmillanSpecialMarkets@macmillan.com.

ISBN 978-1-250-14325-9 (paperback)

Originally published in Australia in 2016 by Pan Macmillan Australia Pty Ltd

First published in the United States by Feiwel and Friends,
an imprint of Macmillan

First Square Fish Edition: 2017
Square Fish logo designed by Filomena Tuosto

10 9 8 7 6 5 4 3

Hi, I'm Andy.

I like to write.

I like to draw.

I like animals.
I also like solving
problems and
doing puzzles.

I like cat
food, cuddles,
cats on TV,
and Jill.

DRAW YOURSELF

Now it's your turn. Draw yourself and write your name.

Hi, I'm

Draw your pet, too, if you have one. If you don't, you could draw one you would like to have.

DRAW SOMETHING YOU LIKE

Draw something you like or something you like to do.

I like _____

DRAW SOMETHING YOU DON'T LIKE

Draw something you don't like or something you don't like to do.

I don't like

DRAW WHERE YOU LIVE

LIST NEW TREEHOUSE LEVELS

We are looking for suggestions for new levels for the treehouse. Any ideas?

PLANS FOR OUR TREEHOUSE

Write your ideas down there... as many as you can.

My ideas for new treehouse levels

Write
your ideas
up there.

13

DRAW NEW TREEHOUSE LEVELS

PLAN YOUR TREEHOUSE VISIT

There is a lot of fun stuff to do in our treehouse. Here are 13 things you can do. What order—from 1 to 13—would you do them in?

comic reading

marshmallow eating

pillow fighting

inventing

swinging

swimming

skating

bowling

Bowling Ball

Andy's Head

driving

VAROOM

baby-dinosaur petting

chocolate waterfalling

lemonade drinking

Dinosaur Egg.

Idiot!

X-raying

WRITE YOUR TO-DO LIST

Write your list down there.

What's on **your** TO-DO list?

Do

Do

Do

Doo-doo!

Doo-doo!

WRITE YOUR TO-DON'T LIST

Write your list
down there.

What's on
your
TO-DON'T list?

Don't

Don't

Don't

Don't-don't!

That's not
funny.

ICE CREAM TIME

Let's go get
an ice cream.

Great idea,
Andy!

Oh no! Some of the
ice cream flavors
are missing!

Professor
Stupido must have
un-invented them.

Let's get the
reader to invent
some new ones.

Great idea,
Jill!

DRAW NEW ICE CREAM FLAVORS

FLYING TIME

DOT-TO-DOT FUN

Once I drew a dot-to-dot rocket for Andy to fill in, but he's not very good at counting so his rocket looked like this.

It was REALLY hard!

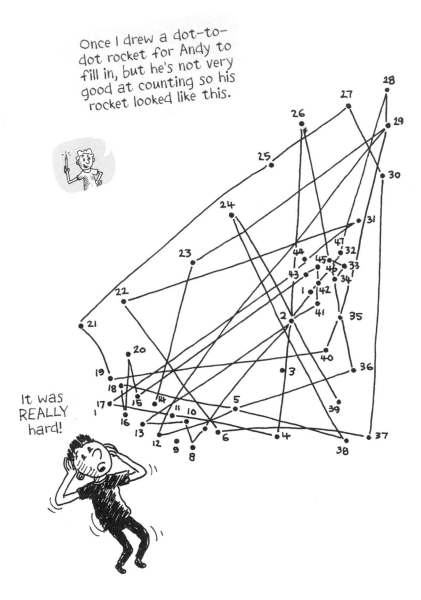

See if you can join the dots to make a better dot-to-dot rocket than Andy.

Good luck! It's not easy.

I'll do it!

COUNT US DOWN

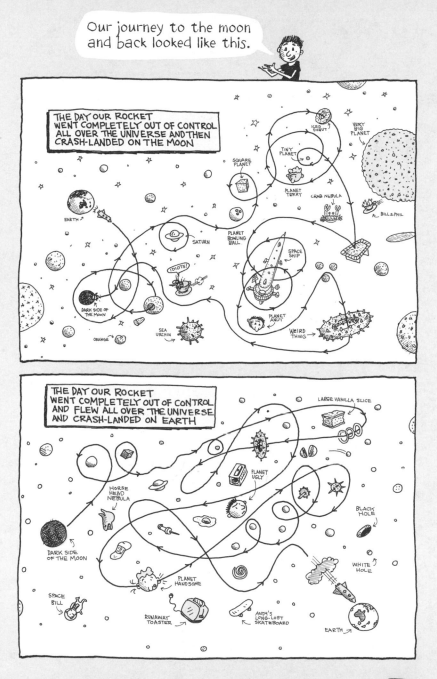

DRAW YOUR SPACE JOURNEY

What does your space journey look like? Where did you go? What did you fly past? Did you crash?

SPOT THE DIFFERENCE

Can you spot 13 differences between these pictures?

Answers are on
page 152.

DRAW OUR SHARKS

UN-INVENT SOMETHING

What would you get
Professor Stupido
to un-invent? Write
it in his poem.

And draw
it, too.

Roses are red,
Violets are blue.
I don't like

_____

So I un-invent you.

BARKY TIME

SPOT THE DIFFERENCE

Can you spot 13 differences between these pictures?

Answers are on page 153.

WRITE SOME WARNING SIGNS

ESCAPE THE MAZE OF DOOM
(IF YOU CAN!)

Can you find your
way out of this maze
or are you doomed?

The answer is
on page 154.

YOU ARE
HERE

ENLARGING TIME

13-STORY TREEHOUSE WORD SEARCH

When you have finished there should be 13 letters left over that spell out something to do with the story.

Answers are on page 155.

WORD LIST

BANANA
BATHROOM
BOWLING
CATAPULT
CHAOS

EGGS
KITCHEN
LABORATORY
MONKEY
NOISE

PAWS
SEA MONKEYS
SWINGING
VINES

S	E	A	M	O	N	K	E	Y	S
C	G	A	N	A	N	A	B	R	W
A	N	S	M	O	O	B	N	O	I
T	I	N	G	K	I	A	V	T	N
A	L	E	S	G	S	T	I	A	G
P	W	H	W	E	E	H	N	R	I
U	O	C	A	Y	M	R	E	O	N
L	B	T	P	A	D	O	S	B	G
T	N	I	C	H	A	O	S	A	E
Y	E	K	N	O	M	M	S	L	S

SOLUTION: _ _ _ _ _ _   _ _ _ _ _ _ _

COLOR IN JILL'S HOUSE

PIZZA TIME

DRAW YOUR OWN PIZZA

Draw your toppings.

What are you going to put on yours?

Pizza dough

ANIMAL PIZZAS

 Animals really love pizza, too.

What pizza do you think these animals would order?

26-STORY TREEHOUSE
WORD SEARCH

```
W  O  O  D  E  N  H  E  A  D
I  T  O  I  D  U  T  S  L  U
C  A  L  O  O  P  C  N  O  M
E  T  S  L  L  U  A  R  Z  U
C  T  E  S  U  C  P  H  N  D
R  O  T  K  E  B  T  Y  O  F
E  O  A  A  Z  K  U  M  G  I
A  Y  R  T  A  P  R  E  R  G
M  I  I  E  M  R  E  A  O  H
T  S  P  L  A  T  D  E  G  T
```

WORD LIST

BULL	MUD FIGHT	STUDIO
CAPTURED	PIRATES	TATTOO
GORGONZOLA	POOL	RHYME
ICE CREAM	SKATE	WOODENHEAD
MAZE	SPLAT	

When you have finished there should be 13 letters left over that spell out something to do with the story.

Answers are on page 156.

SOLUTION: _ _ _ _ _ _ _   _ _ _ _ _ _

54

COLOR IN THE SHARK TANK

DRAWING TIME

I've drawn a worm.
It looks like this.

Yum!

Yum!

What is
that?

My worm
drawing looks
like this.

?

?

DRAW A WORM

DRAW A BANANA

BA·NA·NA
BA·NA·NA

59

COLOR IN CHEESELAND

39-STORY TREEHOUSE
WORD SEARCH

When you have finished there should be 12 letters left over that spell out something to do with the story.

WORD LIST

ANDY	SILKY	UNINVENT
BEETROOT	SPOONCIL	VOLCANO
CHOCOLATE	STUPIDO	WATERFALL
MOON	TERRY	
ROCKET	TRAMPOLINE	

Answers are on page 157.

T	R	A	M	P	O	L	I	N	E
W	E	T	A	L	O	C	O	H	C
A	V	T	O	O	R	T	E	E	B
T	O	S	P	O	O	N	C	I	L
E	L	M	S	L	A	P	A	Y	R
R	C	O	S	L	A	P	N	K	O
F	A	O	S	L	A	P	D	L	C
A	N	N	T	E	R	R	Y	I	K
L	O	D	I	P	U	T	S	S	E
L	U	N	I	N	V	E	N	T	T

SOLUTION: _ _ _ _   _ _ _ _   _ _ _ _

TATTOO TIME

We're getting tattoos from our Automatic Tattoo Machine.

DESIGN YOUR OWN TATTOO

What would you like the ATM to tattoo on you? Draw it.

SPOT THE DIFFERENCE

Can you spot 13 differences between these pictures?

Answers are on page 158.

BARKY, THE BARKING DOG AT THE BEACH

SUPERFINGER TIME

Terry and I invented a character called Superfinger.

Once upon a time there was a finger. But it was no ordinary finger...it was a Superfinger!

Superfinger solves problems that need finger-based solutions—he can help you tie a bow, point you in the right direction, and help you clear a blocked nose. Any time you need an extra finger, Superfinger is there!

CREATE A SUPERHERO

Draw your own superhero.

THE ADVENTURES OF

SUPER_____

What can your superhero do?
_____
_____
_____
_____

REMEMBERING TIME

I REMEMBER ...

Write down some stuff you remember.

A fun holiday I had was

A time I was embarrassed was

A funny thing that happened to me was

I've forgotten what I've forgotten.

A time I was really scared was

TREEHOUSE TRIVIA

Andy and Terry's high-tech detective agency has some pretty high-tech security, including a really hard trivia quiz.

Mmm... that is REALLY hard.

It's you!

And you!

How many of these trivia questions can you answer?

1. What is the name of the sea monster Terry fell in love with?

2. What is the worst job Andy and Terry ever had?

3. What is Terry's favorite TV show?

4. What color did Terry paint Silky?

5. What is the name of Andy and Terry's publisher?

6. What is the name of the pirate who captured Andy, Terry, and me?

7. How many flavors of ice cream are there in Edward Scooperhands' ice-cream parlor?

Answers are on page 159.

MISSING PET POSTER

Make your own missing pet poster. It could be for a pet you have or a made-up one.

MISSING PET!

Likes:

Dislikes:

BIG REWARD!!

SPOT THE DIFFERENCE

Can you spot 13 differences between these pictures?

Answers are on page 160.

52-STORY TREEHOUSE
WORD SEARCH

When you have finished there should be 13 letters left over that spell out something to do with the story.

Answers are on page 161.

WORD LIST

ANDY
BIG
BUTTERFLY
DETECTIVES
DISGUISE

EGGPLANT
NINJA
NOSE
PATTY
POTATO

PRINCE
REMEMBER
SNAILS
TERRY

D	E	T	E	C	T	I	V	E	S
E	P	E	C	N	I	R	P	Y	E
G	O	N	B	I	G	D	A	L	R
G	T	S	O	T	V	I	P	F	E
P	A	N	N	S	E	S	A	R	M
L	T	A	I	Y	E	G	T	E	E
A	O	I	N	D	G	U	T	T	M
N	E	L	J	N	T	I	Y	T	B
T	A	S	A	A	B	S	L	U	E
E	T	E	R	R	Y	E	S	B	R

SOLUTION: _ _ _   _ _ _ _ _ _ _ _ _ _

VEGETABLE COLORING TIME

MIXED-UP ANIMALS

Mix two animals together to create a new one.

PET MAKEOVER TIME

I love creating hairdos for
animals in my pet salon. Why don't
you invent some for all these
animals wanting a new look?

I like curls.

Ssssomething
ssssimple,
pleassse.

Me first!
Do me first!

I'm not sure
what I want.
You choose.

I'm ready
for a big
change. And
I mean BIG!

I feel a change coming on.

Me want hairdo... and ears!

SPOT THE DIFFERENCE

Answers are on page 162.

EXPLODING TIME

There are a lot of explosions in our books. Here are two of my favorites.

THE DAY GORGONZOLA EXPLODED

KABLAM!

THE DAY THE BIGNOSEASAUR EXPLODED

DRAW AN EXPLOSION

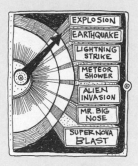

I've set the disaster dial to EXPLOSION so now it's your turn to draw one.

ANIMAL SCRAMBLES

My animals' names are all mixed up. Can you fix them?

RM EEH WAH

_____

EMO

_____

SLIYK

_____

Answers are on page 163.

LRARY

BLLI & PILH

TAP

SCREECHY COLOR IN

Color in the screechy picture.

65-STORY TREEHOUSE
WORD SEARCH

When you have finished there should be eight letters left over that spell out something to do with the story.

Answers are on page 164.

WORD LIST

ANTS	CRAB	OWLS	SELFIE
ASPS	EGYPT	PERMIT	SUPER BW
BIN	FIRE	POND SCUM	TIME TRAVEL
BUBBLE WRAP	INSPECTOR	RAMPS	TREE NN
CLONING			

```
B  G  S  B  T  P  Y  G  E  L
U  N  U  A  S  B  I  N  P  E
B  I  P  R  N  E  R  I  F  V
B  N  E  C  O  T  L  O  P  A
L  O  R  P  S  O  S  F  O  R
E  L  B  L  P  E  R  M  I  T
W  C  W  T  R  E  E  N  N  E
R  O  T  C  E  P  S  N  I  M
A  S  P  S  S  P  M  A  R  I
P  O  N  D  S  C  U  M  P  T
```

SOLUTION: _ _ _ _   _ _ _ _

FIND THE ODD ONE OUT

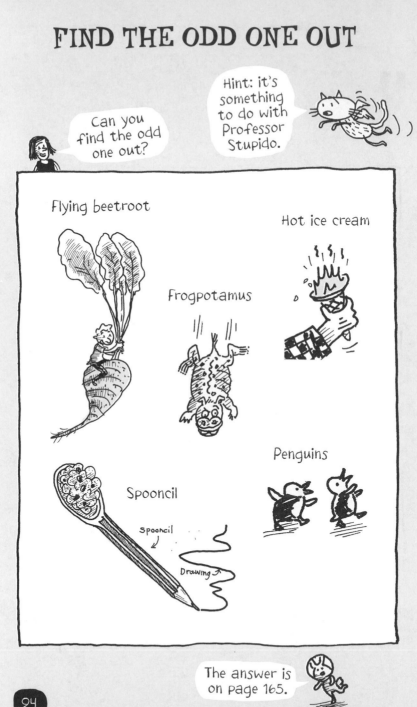

SOUND EFFECTS FUN

Un-inventing is very noisy. Fill the page with as many different sound effects as you can.

BLEEP!

VEGETABLE DISGUISE TIME

COLOR THIS IN ... OR ELSE!

ADVERTISEMENT TIME

These are advertisements I did for two of my inventions.

Create your own advertisement for a product you'd like to invent.

VAPORIZING VEGETABLES TIME

FEEDING TIME

Terry and I have a marshmallow machine that automatically shoots marshmallows into our mouths whenever we're hungry.

 If you had a machine like this what food would you like it to feed you? Draw it.

SAFETY TIME

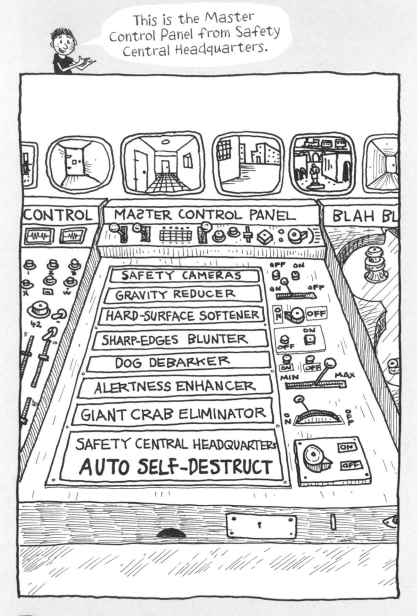

WHAT'S CHASING ANDY?

WHAT'S CHASING TERRY?

FUN FOOD LEVEL

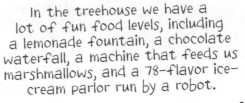

In the treehouse we have a lot of fun food levels, including a lemonade fountain, a chocolate waterfall, a machine that feeds us marshmallows, and a 78-flavor ice-cream parlor run by a robot.

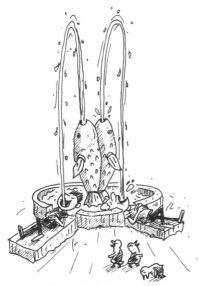

LEMONADE FOUNTAIN

CHOCOLATE WATERFALL

MARSHMALLOW MACHINE

ICE-CREAM PARLOR

STORY TIME

I like stories with lots of action.

I like nonsense and random stuff.

COLOR IN THE CRASH

COLOR IN THE COVER

TREEHOUSE CODE TIME

A
B
C
D
E

F
G
H
I
J

K
L
M
N
O

P
Q
R
S
T

U
V
W
X

Y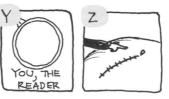
YOU, THE READER
Z

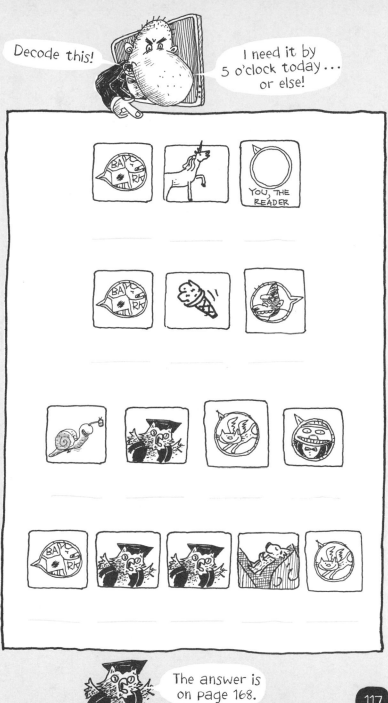

The answer is on page 170.

FIND-THE-UNICORN FUN

I can't remember where I put it... lucky the answer is on page 171.

121

THE REALLY HUNGRY
CATERPILLAR'S STORY

Fill in the blanks
and color the
pictures to tell
my story.

The really hungry caterpillar

ate one _ _ _ _ _ _ _

f r i e d - _ _ _

_ _ _

_ _ _ _ enormous

black bird .

two

_ _ _ _ _ _ rhinoceroses

_ _ _ _ _ wacky waving

inflatable _ _ _ _ -

flailing _ _ _ _ _ men

five giant mutant

_ _ _ _ _ _ _

one grumpy old

_ _ _ _ _ _

one wall of

_ _ _ _ _ _ _ _

spears

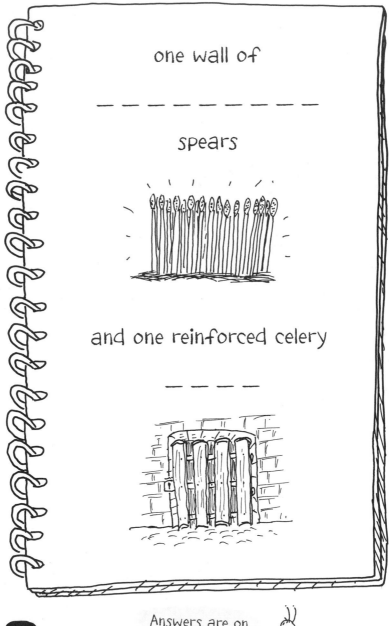

and one reinforced celery

_ _ _ _ _

126

Answers are on pages 172–174.

WHAT FAIRY TALE IS THAT?

Can you tell what stories these are?

Two children, lost in the woods,
find a house made of gingerbread.

H _ _ _ _ _

_ N _

_ _ _ _ _ L

While walking through the woods to Grandmother's house, a young child encounters a wolf.

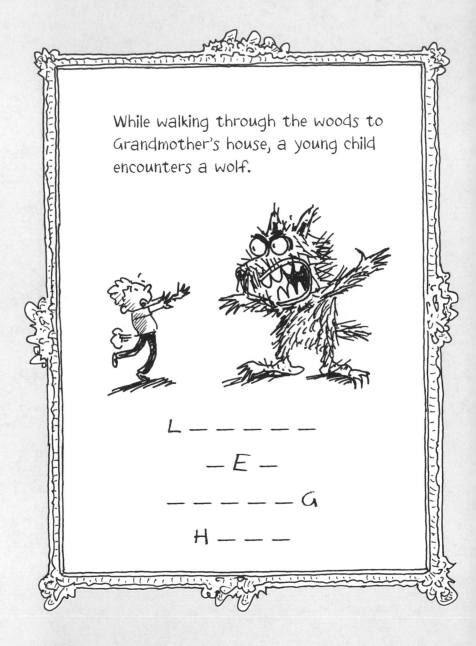

L _ _ _ _ _ _

_ E _

_ _ _ _ _ G

H _ _ _

Prince Charming travels throughout his kingdom trying to find the owner of the golden slipper.

C _ _ _ _ _ _ _ L _ _

Answers are on page 175.

WHO REALLY SAID WHAT?!

 These quotes are all mixed up. Draw a line from the speech bubble to the character who REALLY said it.

TERRY

That's crazy! SO crazy it just might work!

BARKY
THE BARKING DOG

The sharks are sick! They ate my underpants!

ANDY

BARK! BARK! BARK! BARK! BARK! BARK!

Answers are on page 176.

MR. BIG NOSE

BA–NA–NA!
BA–NA–NA!

JILL

Don't argue!
I'm a busy man—
I don't have time
to argue!

GIANT
GORILLA

You went
off and left
me here all
small.

CANNON-BLASTING TIME

Would you like to blast something out of our cannon?

3.. 2... 1...

BLAM!

Draw what
(or who) it
is flying
through
the air.

Or, maybe,
your teacher...

You could
draw your little
brother...

DINNERTIME

Dinnertime!
Draw a line from
each animal to its
food bowl.

1001 WAYS TO COOK THISTLES

BILL & PHIL

MANNY

SILKY

Answers are on page 177.

PINK

CURLY

MR. HEE-H

LOOMPY

TRAM-RIDE TIME

Continue the tram's journey.

FIND THE ODD ONE OUT

Can you find the odd one out?

Hint: it's something to do with where we live.

MR. HEE-HAW

PAT

SILKY, THE FLYING CAT

BABY DINOSAURS

The answer is on page 178.

MOE

TREE-COLORING TIME

TREEHOUSE TRUE OR FALSE?

Mark the boxes to show if these statements are true or false.

T F

1. Silky is my favorite pet.

2. Mr. Big Nose has a very bad temper.

3. Ninja Snails move very quickly.

4. Andy and Terry live in a 13-story motor home.

5. I live in a house full of animals.

6. Andy and Terry love vegetables.

7. Bill the postman is a policeman.

8. Terry painted Silky yellow.

9. The Trunkinator is a boxing elephant.

10. Andy and Terry once worked in the monkey house at the zoo.

11. ATM stands for Automatic Tea Machine.

12. Prince Potato really likes Andy and Terry and is happy to spend time with them.

13. The treehouse has a see-through swimming pool.

Answers are on page 179.

FIND THE ODD ONE OUT

Can you find the odd one out? I'll give you a hint—it's not me!

ANDY

TERRY

EDWARD
SCOOPERHANDS

MR. BIG NOSE

The answer is on page 180.

BILL
THE POSTMAN

TREEHOUSE CROSSWORD

Use the clues to fill in the crossword.

ACROSS

1. He writes the words
3. He draws the pictures
7. Very wise animals that live in the treehouse
9. Short for Automatic Tattoo Machine
10. What Terry is training his snails to be
14. Andy and Terry have a Flying Fried-Egg __ __ __
15. He's a postman

DOWN

1. They live in the ant farm
2. Andy and Terry have a Maze of __ __ __ __
4. Andy and Terry have a Rocking Horse
   __ __ __ __   __ __ __ __ __
5. The part of the Flying Fried-Egg Car that Andy and Terry sit in
6. Terry's second favorite TV show is *Buzzy the Buzzing* __ __ __
8. What Andy wants to do in every contest
11. Andy and Terry's neighbor and friend
12. Jill's pet cat
13. What Terry and Andy live in

Answers are on page 181.

DRAW ANDY IN DANGER

I love drawing pictures of Andy in terrible danger. Help me finish these ones by drawing over the lines in the pictures of the dangerous animals.

I can't watch this.

Me neither!

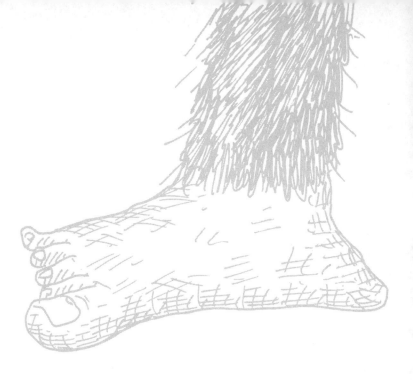

Be quiet, Barky, I'm trying to read.

BARK!

That's weird ...I can smell elephant.

Dinnertime!

CATAPULT FUN

What would you like to get rid of? Draw it in our giant catapult.

ANTIGRAVITY TIME

 All this writing,
drawing and puzzle
solving has been fun,
but I'm exhausted.

Me too. Let's go
for a nice, relaxing
float in the
antigravity chamber.

 But I'm too
tired to draw
us in there.

Why don't we
ask the readers
to do it?

 Great idea,
Jill!

151

ANSWER TIME

SPOT THE DIFFERENCE (PAGES 32–33)

ESCAPE THE MAZE OF DOOM (PAGE 46)

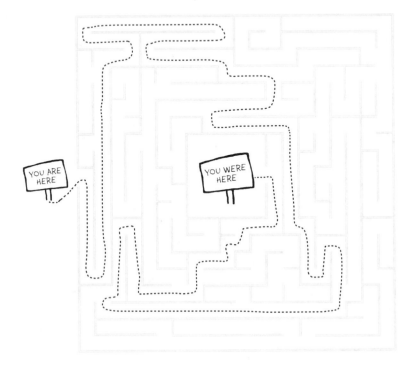

13-STORY TREEHOUSE WORD SEARCH (PAGE 48)

S	E	A	M	O	N	K	E	Y	S
C	G	A	N	A	N	A	B	R	W
A	N	S	M	O	O	B	N	O	I
T	I	N	G	K	I	A	V	T	N
A	L	E	S	G	S	T	I	A	G
P	W	H	W	E	E	H	N	R	I
U	O	C	A	Y	M	R	E	O	N
L	B	T	P	A	D	O	S	B	G
T	N	I	C	H	A	O	S	A	E
Y	E	K	N	O	M	M	S	L	S

Solution: MONKEY MADNESS

26-STORY TREEHOUSE WORD SEARCH (PAGE 54)

W	O	O	D	E	N	H	E	A	D
I	T	O	I	D	U	T	S	L	U
C	A	L	O	O	P	C	N	O	M
E	T	S	L	L	U	A	R	Z	U
C	T	E	S	U	C	P	H	N	D
R	O	T	K	E	B	T	Y	O	F
E	O	A	A	Z	K	U	M	G	I
A	Y	R	T	A	P	R	E	R	G
M	I	I	E	M	R	E	A	O	H
T	S	P	L	A	T	D	E	G	T

Solution: UNLUCKY PIRATE

Eeeee-yaahhhhhhhhh!

156

T	R	A	M	P	O	L	I	N	E
W	E	T	A	L	O	C	O	H	C
A	V	T	O	O	R	T	E	E	B
T	O	S	P	O	O	N	C	I	L
E	L	M	S	L	A	P	A	Y	R
R	C	O	S	L	A	P	N	K	O
F	A	O	S	L	A	P	D	L	C
A	N	N	T	E	R	R	Y	I	K
L	O	D	I	P	U	T	S	S	E
L	U	N	I	N	V	E	N	T	T

Solution: SLAP! SLAP! SLAP!

1. What is the name of the sea monster Terry fell in love with?

   Mermaidia

2. What is the worst job Andy and Terry ever had?

   Filling in for the monkeys at the zoo

3. What is Terry's favorite TV show?

   The Barky the Barking Dog Show

4. What color did Terry paint Silky?

   Yellow

5. What is the name of Andy and Terry's publisher?

   Mr. Big Nose

6. What is the name of the pirate who captured Andy, Terry, and me?

   Captain Woodenhead

7. How many flavors of ice cream are there in Edward Scooperhands' ice-cream parlor?

   78

D	E	T	E	C	T	I	V	E	S
E	P	E	C	N	I	R	P	Y	E
G	O	N	B	I	G	D	A	L	R
G	T	S	O	T	V	I	P	F	R
P	A	N	N	S	E	S	A	R	M
L	T	A	I	Y	E	G	T	E	E
A	O	I	N	D	G	U	T	T	M
N	E	L	J	N	T	I	Y	T	B
T	A	S	A	A	B	S	L	U	E
E	T	E	R	R	Y	E	S	B	R

Solution: EAT VEGETABLES

ANIMAL SCRAMBLES (PAGES 90–91)

RM EEH WAH

MR. HEE HAW

EMO

MOE

SLIYK

SILKY

LRARY

LARRY

BLLI & PILH

BILL & PHIL

TAP

PAT

65-STORY TREEHOUSE WORD SEARCH (PAGE 93)

B	G	S	B	T	P	Y	G	E	L
U	N	U	A	S	B	I	N	P	E
B	I	P	R	N	E	R	I	F	V
B	N	E	C	O	T	L	O	P	A
L	O	R	P	S	O	S	F	O	R
E	L	B	L	P	E	R	M	I	T
W	C	W	T	R	E	E	N	N	E
R	O	T	C	E	P	S	N	I	M
A	S	P	S	S	P	M	A	R	I
P	O	N	D	S	C	U	M	P	T

Solution: POOP-POOP

CHICKEN! CHUTNEY! POOP-POOP!

FIND THE ODD ONE OUT (PAGE 94)

Flying beetroot

Hot ice cream

Frogpotamus

Spooncil

Spooncil

Drawing

Penguins

Answer: Spooncil.
It's the only one Professor Stupido didn't un-invent.

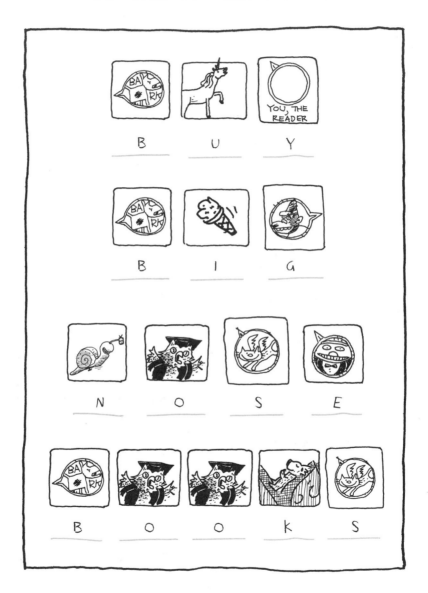

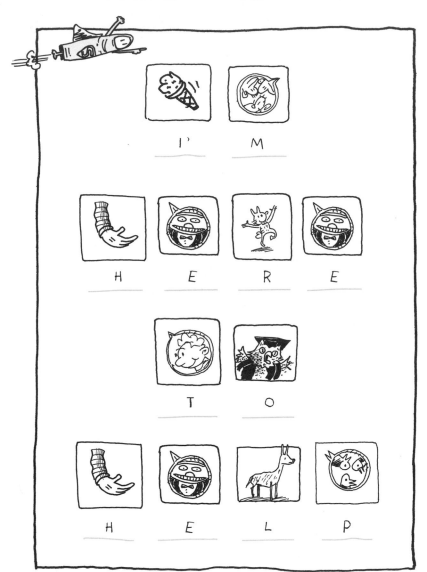

I'   M

H   E   R   E

T   O

H   E   L   P

FIND-THE-UNICORN FUN (PAGES 120–121)

THE REALLY HUNGRY CATERPILLAR'S STORY (PAGES 122–126)

PAGE 122

The really hungry caterpillar

ate one F L Y I N G

fried-E G G

C A R

PAGE 123

O N E enormous

black bird

PAGE 123

two

S T E A M R O L L E R S

PAGE 124

T H R E E rhinoceroses

PAGE 124

F O U R wacky waving

inflatable A R M -

flailing T U B E men

PAGE 125

five giant mutant

S P I D E R S

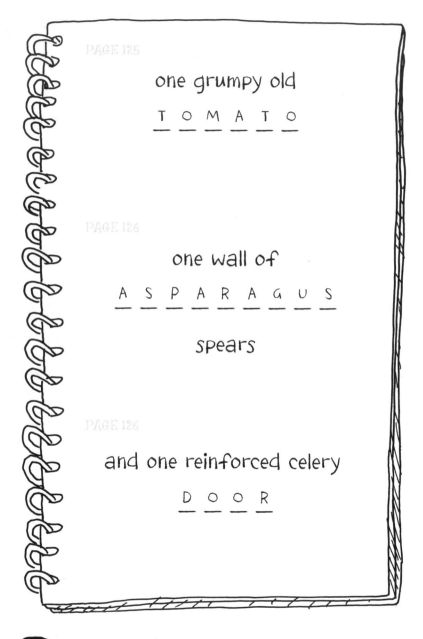

one grumpy old

T O M A T O

one wall of

A S P A R A G U S

spears

and one reinforced celery

D O O R

PAGE 127

HANSEL AND GRETEL

PAGE 128

LITTLE RED RIDING HOOD

PAGE 129

CINDERELLA

TERRY — The sharks are sick! They ate my underpants!

BARKY THE BARKING DOG — BARK! BARK! BARK! BARK! BARK! BARK!

ANDY — That's crazy! SO crazy it just might work!

MR. BIG NOSE — Don't argue! I'm a busy man— I don't have time to argue!

JILL — You went off and left me here all small.

GIANT GORILLA — BA-NA-NA! BA-NA-NA!

DINNERTIME (PAGES 134–135)

FIND THE ODD ONE OUT (PAGE 138)

Answer: The baby dinosaurs are the odd ones out.
They live in the treehouse, but all the other animals
live at Jill's house.

MR. HEE-HAW

PAT

SILKY,
THE FLYING CAT

BABY
DINOSAURS

MOE

TREEHOUSE TRUE OR FALSE? (PAGE 140)

T F

☑ ☐   1. Silky is my favorite pet.

☑ ☐   2. Mr. Big Nose has a very bad temper.

☐ ☑   3. Ninja Snails move very quickly.

☐ ☑   4. Andy and Terry live in a 13-story motor home.

☑ ☐   5. I live in a house full of animals.

☐ ☑   6. Andy and Terry love vegetables.

☐ ☑   7. Bill the postman is a policeman.

☑ ☐   8. Terry painted Silky yellow.

☑ ☐   9. The Trunkinator is a boxing elephant.

☑ ☐   10. Andy and Terry once worked in the monkey house at the zoo.

☐ ☑   11. ATM stands for Automatic Tea Machine.

☐ ☑   12. Prince Potato really likes Andy and Terry and is happy to spend time with them.

☑ ☐   13. The treehouse has a see-through swimming pool.

FIND THE ODD ONE OUT (PAGE 141)

Answer: Edward Scooperhands is the odd one out. He is a robot, but all the others are human beings.

TREEHOUSE CROSSWORD (PAGES 142–143)

A	N	D	Y		T	E	R	R	Y
N		O		F		A			O
T		O	W	L	S		C		L
S		M		Y			E		K
	W					A	T	M	
N	I	N	J	A	S		R		
	N		I		I		A		T
			L		L		C	A	R
B	I	L	L		K		K		E
					Y				E

Andy Griffiths lives in an amazing treehouse with his friend Terry and together they make funny books, just like the one you're holding in your hands right now. Andy writes the words and Terry draws the pictures. If you'd like to know more, read the Treehouse series (or visit www.andygriffiths.com.au).

Terry Denton lives in an amazing treehouse with his friend Andy and together they make funny books, just like the one you're holding in your hands right now. Terry draws the pictures and Andy writes the words. If you'd like to know more, read the Treehouse series (or visit www.terrydenton.com).

Jill Griffiths lives near Andy and Terry in a house full of animals. She has two dogs, one goat, three horses, four goldfish, one cow, two guinea pigs, one camel, one donkey, thirteen cats, and so many rabbits she has lost count. If you'd like to know more, read the Treehouse series.